SHARING MY ALLURING HOT WIFE

WIFE SHARING HOTWIFE EROTICA COLLECTION

WIFE SHARING FANTASIES
BOOK ONE

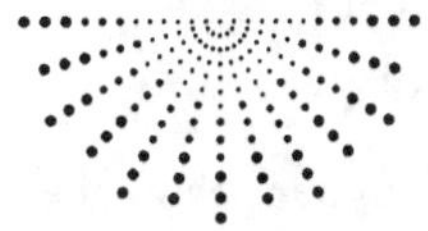

LEE RILEY

* * *

* * *

 Created with Vellum

SHARING MY WIFE WITH CO-WORKERS

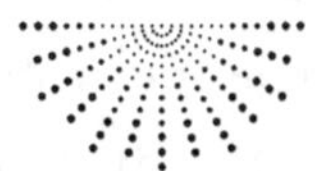

* * *

The rope was starting to chafe my wrists, and with Aiden's silk tie acting as a blindfold there was nothing to distract me from it.

Okay, that's not entirely true.

He had left me naked in the backyard when the doorbell rang. The pain from the shiny silver nipple clamps hanging from my lush breasts had finally reduced down to a dull throb. It matched the ache in my shoulders from having my arms stretched apart over my head for so long. The ropes binding my wrists were looped through the wooden slats of the pergola that shaded our patio, and the rough cement I was kneeling on was pleasantly cool given how hot the day was.

I could have distracted myself by focusing on any of those sensations. Being deprived of sight made all my other senses pretty keen. Especially hearing. But I tuned out the voices and laughter coming from inside the house and turned my attention back to my uncomfortable wrists. I had to remember to ask him if we could get some leather cuffs.

Aiden had made no effort to hide me, and anyone who happened to walk into the kitchen and look out the sliding glass doors would have seen me. I wondered if that had already happened.

When Aiden and I started dating, our sex life was pretty tame. Nice, definitely, but nothing more than your standard fucking and a bit of oral. Things started to change once we got engaged, and I blame it on his friend Bruce.

Aiden met Bruce at the gym shortly after the other man moved to town. The two hit it off, and went from being work out buddies to barbecuing together on the weekends and getting together for drinks a few times during the week.

I really like Bruce's wife, Ava. Although she does seem ridiculously young. They've only been married about a year longer than we have, and are blissfully happy. Right after Aiden proposed, the four of us were drinking and barbecuing here in the backyard, and I asked Ava what their secret was.

"Spanking!" she blurted out, and then blushed furiously.

She tried to play it off as a joke, but later, Bruce pulled Aiden aside and talked to him about their Domestic Discipline lifestyle.

"Of course they're blissfully happy, angel," Aiden laughed as he told me about it later. "Ava does whatever he wants, and if she doesn't, he gets to bend her over his knee and spank her!"

That night, he playfully pushed me down on the bed when we were getting undressed and gave me a few swats on the ass. I laughed, thinking it was all pretty silly, but Aiden…

I guess some desires can lie dormant inside people, so quietly that they don't even realize they're there. Aiden had never spanked anyone before, but that first spontaneous interlude showed him something about himself.

He started spanking me more often, and much harder. All part of sex play, and I didn't mind. Much. Because it *really* turned him on. But then he decided that he wanted to take it further.

The sound of the sliding glass door opening startled me, and I jerked my wrists ineffectively against the rough rope. My heart started racing and I struggled to listen over the rush of blood in my ears. Was it just my husband?

I heard the sound of heavy breathing. Of course. Someone was staring at me, naked and spread before them like a willing sex slave. Which, of course, is exactly what I had become.

Two. There were two people breathing. I wondered if one of them was Aiden, or if he had sent two of his friends out of their own.

"Holy shit," one of them whispered. He kept his voice too low for me to tell whether I recognized it.

"Go ahead. She doesn't bite."

That one was Aiden. So he'd brought someone out to use me. The heavy breathing got even louder as the sound of a zipper coming down sounded right in front of my face. Then rough hands in my hair.

"Careful! Don't loosen the blindfold or we have to stop playing," Aiden chuckled at the other man's eagerness.

A hard cock was pressed against my lips, and when I parted them and touched the tip with my tongue he sucked in a quick breath and tightened his hands on my head.

"Oh my God!" Still in a whisper. I wondered if it was someone I knew.

I'd been trained well, and I opened my lips wide without any urging and sucked the length of him into my warm, wet mouth. He wasn't overly long, but nice and thick.

Every man has his own unique scent, and as I worked this cock in and out of my mouth, swallowing it down my throat and making him groan, I was almost positive that I'd never had this one before.

My cheeks, jaw, and throat had become incredibly strong, and it wasn't long before his excitement at what I was doing made him rough. He started slamming into my face, his soft pubic hair rubbing against my nose and cheeks, and if I hadn't had so much practice it would have made me gag. As it was, I could tell the minute he was about to come.

"Fuck! Fuck! Fuckfuckfuckfuck*fuccckkkkkk!!!!!!!*"

His thick cock swelled even larger for a moment before he ground himself into my face and pumped jets of hot, salty cum down my throat. He held me so tightly, for so long, that I started to struggle for air.

Suddenly he was pulled away from me, his softening cock slopping against my chin and leaving a wet smear under my lips.

"Don't suffocate my wife, Jer," Aiden said with a laugh.

"Sorry, man. Fuck! She's a fucking vacuum cleaner!"

Jer. Jerry. It must be the new guy in his office, the young one fresh out of college that they'd hired a couple of weeks ago. My cheeks burned. My husband was my master, and in his wisdom he always blindfolded me. I readily consented to being used, but I'd rather not know by who.

"Let's get back before we're missed," Aiden said to the younger man. "We don't want the rest of the team to get jealous that you got a preview of coming attractions."

As I heard one set of footsteps head back to the house my husband leaned down and whispered in my ear.

"We may be awhile, angel, but I haven't forgotten about you. Now be a good girl and stay quiet."

He kissed my forehead, and reached down to remove my nipple clamps. *Shit!*

"Take a deep breath, Mila," he ordered.

He unclamped me without any further warning, and it took everything I had not to scream as the blood rushed back into my little peaks like a tsunami of pain. Panting, I held it in, and was rewarded with his tongue softly swirling over my oversensitized nipples for a moment.

"I'll be back," he promised.

By the time my nipples had calmed down, my arms were numb. The house was pretty quiet, and I wondered if everyone had left. The glass door finally slid open again and I heard Aiden's footsteps.

"I'm sorry we were interrupted earlier, angel," he whispered as he pulled on the ropes to raise me up off my knees. "I had no idea the guys from the office were going to get here early."

I didn't answer, of course. I knew better.

When Aiden had finally convinced me that we should practice Domestic Discipline in our marriage, the way Ava and Bruce did, I had agreed in part because I thought it was just his excuse to justify more spanking games.

I didn't take the idea of submitting to his authority all that seriously at first. Yes, he could be the Head of Household and I would be his obedient wife. Yes, he should punish me if I broke his rules or needed my behavior "corrected". I agreed to all that. I just didn't realize that we had very different things in mind.

What I saw as another kind of role playing sex game, Aiden saw as an excuse to unleash the beast that his first taste of spanking me had awakened in him. He got off on dominating me, and I played along at first. I didn't even protest when he wanted to punish me the first time I broke one of his house rules.

Of course, I was picturing his punishment as another round of bare bottom spanking followed by hot, steamy sex.

"What's *that* for, honey?" I'd laughed when he brought out the rope.

"I need to make sure that you don't move during your punishment, Mila." He was so serious. I played along. I got up on the bed on all fours as directed, and laughed when he pushed my chest down with a hand between my shoulder blades.

"Reach through your legs and grab your ankles, Mila," he'd ordered.

As soon as I was in the position he wanted, he started lashing my ankles and wrists together. Tightly.

"Ow! Not so snug, please," I pouted.

Instead of laughing along with me, he smacked my ass. Hard.

"Ow!" I cried out. "Aiden, that's not funny."

"Mila, you will not speak again during your punishment, or it will go much worse for you."

He had my hands and feet bound tightly together by then, and having my arms stretched out under my body put a little strain on my shoulders and forced my ass up into an easily accessible position.

Aiden ran an extra piece of rope around my left knee, and, tugging it hard so that my leg spread open, he tied it to the bed frame. Once he'd repeated that on my other side I was spread wide and completely vulnerable, and my heart was hammering in my chest.

"This feels a little scary, honey," I told him honestly.

Smack! His hand cracked against my ass again. My skin was stretched taut, and it felt like fire.

"Quiet."

He left the room for a minute, and I lay there trying to figure out if we were playing. Because it didn't feel like we were playing. I felt like I was completely at his mercy.

My heart stuttered for a moment at the thought. And then I smiled. I liked it.

He walked back in carrying a… what the fuck was it? Some kind of *whip*? My husband was holding onto a black leather handle with a series of short, knotted leather strips hanging from it.

"What the fuck, Aiden!"

He didn't answer, just walked around behind me and started flailing the leather tool against my ass and thighs. This was nothing like our sexy play spankings. Some of those had left me red and stinging, but this… stripes of fire were ripping across my tender skin, and every few strikes one of those venomous strips would flick against my pussy and make me scream.

He had me bound so tightly that I couldn't move, and I started bawling, my mascara running into my eyes until they stung and snot clogging my nose. I don't know how long he whipped me that first time, but by the time he stopped my throat was raw and my eyes had swollen so much from crying that I could barely see.

I couldn't see Aiden behind me, but I could hear him breathing heavily.

"You are mine, Mila," he panted. "And you will obey, or be punished."

His words sent a hot thrill through me. I felt the bed dip as he kneeled behind me and grabbed my hips. His touch on my abused flesh made me whimper, but then his cock was in me and my whimper became a moan. He fucked me hard and fast, not even pausing as a massive orgasm ripped through me.

When he finally came, he didn't say a word. He just pulled out and left me, tied up and well used, as he went to clean himself up. It was the most degrading fuck of my life, and shame washed over me as I realized how much I wanted him to do it again.

Something shifted in our relationship after that. He could tell I wanted more, and it stopped being a game. Submitting to his will became instinctive, and the more I submitted, the more he pushed the limits of his ownership.

He started telling me what to wear. And what not to wear.

"No underwear tonight, angel," he would whisper before taking me to dinner. "I want access to my pussy."

Aiden loved to finger me in public places, and I quickly learned not to protest. The first time I did, there were consequences. He would never made a scene in public, but at home he had added a whole series of leather restraints and torturous implements to that first cat o'nine tails whip.

His punishments were immediate, and severe, and only had to be administered once for any offense. I'm a quick learner.

Aiden loved how tame I'd become, and it only made him bolder. He had already spread his dominance into our bedroom, and now he started ordering me to suck him off in public. In the back of a cab. Crawling under the tablecloth at a 5-star restaurant. In an elevator or a dressing room or an unused office in his building.

I became so obedient that I stopped even thinking about it when he gave me a command. I just instinctively did as I was told. Giving up control to someone I love and trust, completely and unconditionally, was a relief. It was freeing.

When my husband realized how completely I'd submitted to him, he started to flaunt his ownership. Giving me blatant orders and shamelessly touching me in front of others. And I loved every minute of it.

I was a little shocked the first time he decided to let another man use me. Before he became my master, Aiden had already been possessive of me. Any attention from other men would have instantly made him jealous, and probably led to a nasty fight.

As soon as I became utterly submissive, his possessiveness evaporated. He *knew* he owned. I was his, body, mind, and spirit. It didn't matter if I had other men's cocks inside me. If Aiden allowed them there, then it only enhanced his power.

I smiled, trying to tell by sound how many men had come out to the patio with him. Aiden hauled me up by my bound wrists until I was dangling upright from the pergola. He must have already told them that I was a reward for the ones who had hit their quarterly bonuses, because immediately one of my legs was lifted by a calloused hand and my pussy fingered roughly.

"Mila, these boys worked hard at the office to earn the right to be here," Aiden told me as the unknown man handled me. "I hope you're wet and ready."

"Yes, sir," I answered dutifully. And I was.

"Fuck, Aiden! She *wants* it!" someone said with a laugh.

But that wasn't true. It wasn't a matter of wanting. It was a matter of submitting. Admitting I wanted this would have been degrading. But submitting gave me permission to be used without remorse.

I gave a small whimper as the man holding me removed his finger and jammed his cock into my hungry pussy. He held one of my legs around his hip and clutched my ass with his other hand, then held me steady and fucked me in front of my husband.

I've had some of the best orgasms of my life while I was tied up. Bondage gives you no choice but to take it, and this man had me at the perfect angle to rub against my clit as he used me.

"Oooooooooooooh," I sighed happily as I came.

The next one asked Aiden to lower my arms so he could bend me over and fuck me from behind. He mounted me like a horse, and slid into my cum filled slit with a groan. This position wasn't nearly as comfortable, and I spread my legs for balance right before a third man stepped in front of me and pushed his cock into my mouth.

Sucking dutifully, I recognized his taste. This one had used me before, although I didn't know his name. He had a skinny cock that curved upward a bit and tickled the roof of my mouth as I serviced him. He was a moaner, and so loud that I almost didn't notice when the one behind me came and was replaced by a fourth.

I came again as I listened to the wet, slurping, smacking sounds men stroking eager cocks. I didn't know how many more were circled around me, watching and waiting for a turn. Some would probably use me more than once, and in multiple holes. I gave up trying to guess how many men my husband had invited over.

I could smell barbecue in the background, and my stomach growled as another man stepped in front of me.

"Careful, Chuck," someone warned. "Sounds like she's hungry."

"I'll give her some meat!" he shouted gleefully as I took his thick cock down my throat. I sucked it greedily. Better than barbecue, anytime.

"Aiden, buddy, I know you promised us that hitting our sales goals would be worth it, but *fuck*! If I'd known *this* was waiting for us I would have doubled it!"

I heard my husband laugh happily. I swear I could *hear* him smiling as he basked in the glow of his team's admiration. Feeling powerful made him horny, and I hoped he had his own cock out. I wanted him to fuck me with his boys before the night was over.

"I'll make you a deal, Eddie," my husband offered once the laughter died down. "If you double your sales next quarter, you can have her to yourself for a week!"

"Fuck, *yeah!*" screamed the man with his cock buried inside me. I couldn't tell if he was responding to my husband's offer or to shooting his load into me. But the idea of being given to someone as their own private sex slave definitely made *me* come. Again.

"Aiden was talking to *me*, Vince," Eddie said as he pulled the other man off of me and took his place. "And I-- *unghhh,* accept-- *unghhh.*"

Me, too! I thought happily as I took another cock, and another, and another.

* * *

SHARING MY WIFE WITH THE MILKMAN

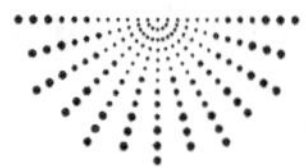

* * *

The early morning sun cast a warm, golden glow through the kitchen window, illuminating the meticulously arranged breakfast nook where Jessie sat, sipping her coffee. The steam danced upwards, mingling with the sunbeams, creating a hazy aura around her. Jessie's gaze drifted outside, lost in the mundane beauty of her perfectly manicured suburban garden. The chirping of birds and the distant hum of the city were the only sounds piercing the serene silence of the morning.

As she placed her cup down, the gentle clink of porcelain against the saucer echoed in the quiet room. She glanced at the clock. It was almost time.

Every Tuesday and Thursday, precisely at 8:30 a.m., Harvey, the milkman, would arrive. Jessie found herself increasingly looking forward to these brief, innocuous encounters. They were a respite from the monotonous routine of her daily life as a housewife.

The sound of a vehicle pulling up broke her reverie. Peering through the window, she saw the familiar white van with bold blue letters: "Harvey's Dairy Products." Her heart fluttered with a mix of excitement and nervous anticipation. Today, she had decided, would be different. Today, she would break the cycle of boredom that had become her life.

As she heard Harvey's footsteps approaching the front door, Jessie quickly adjusted her apron, smoothing out nonexistent creases. She took a deep breath and opened the door with a practiced smile.

"Good morning, Harvey!" she greeted, her voice a little too cheerful.

Harvey, a tall man with a friendly face and a hint of a smile, greeted her back. "Morning, Jessie! Got your usual order here," he said, lifting a crate of milk bottles.

"Thank you, Harvey. Would you mind bringing them in for me? My back has been acting up lately," Jessie said, stepping aside to let him in.

"Of course, no problem at all," Harvey replied, his tone warm and obliging.

As Harvey entered the kitchen, Jessie couldn't help but notice the way his muscles flexed under his uniform when he set down the crate. She bit her lip, a plan forming in her mind.

"Would you like a cup of coffee, Harvey? It's the least I can do for all your help," she offered, her voice laced with a hint of something more, an invitation perhaps.

Harvey looked surprised but pleased. "Well, I shouldn't really... but a quick cup wouldn't hurt, I guess."

As Jessie busied herself making coffee, the aroma of freshly ground beans filled the air. She was acutely aware of Harvey's presence behind her, the air charged with a subtle, unspoken tension.

"So, Harvey, how's life treating you these days?" Jessie asked casually, turning to face him with two steaming cups of coffee.

"It's... it's good, you know, the usual. Just busy with the rounds and all," Harvey answered, accepting the cup.

Jessie smiled, taking a sip of coffee, her eyes never leaving his. "You work so hard, Harvey, I don't know how you do it."

"Oh, it's nothing, really. Just part of the job, I guess," Harvey replied with a shrug.

There was a pause, the silence punctuated only by the sound of their breathing. Jessie sat on her kitchen counter and an idea struck her, one she didn't know if she had the nerve to pull off. But she gathered her nerves and looked Harvey in the eye as she slowly pulled her dress up and spread her knees ever so slightly, just enough to reveal to the handsome milkman that she wasn't wearing any panties.

Harvey's eyes went wide with shock and arousal, and the sudden movement of his hands towards his crotch confirmed her suspicions — he was hard. Jessie felt a rush of power and desire, knowing she had this effect on him.

Harvey was frozen in place, his eyes glued to the forbidden sight of her bare pussy, and Jessie's breath caught in her throat. She couldn't believe she was doing this, exposing herself to a virtual stranger. The thrill of it was intoxicating, and she reveled in the knowledge that she was in control, that she was calling the shots.

As Harvey's gaze burned into her, Jessie felt a surge of arousal course through her veins. She leaned back, her legs spread even wider, and let her fingers trace a path of desire down her neck and chest, finally resting on her breasts.

"My," Jessie let out in a whisper. "It's not even 9 yet and it's so hot. This summer has been unbearable."

"Uh-huh," Harvey mumbled in a daze, still transfixed by the sight of her.

"I'm already sweating like a whore in church," Jessie continued in a husky voice. "Do you mind if I... cool down a little?"

Harvey could only nod, his eyes dark with lust.

Jessie licked her lips and slowly began to unbutton her dress, letting it fall open to reveal her full, milky cleavage. She could see the tent in Harvey's pants growing ever larger, and she felt a delicious thrill of excitement knowing that she was the cause of it.

"I'm feeling a bit faint. Could you come over here and help me?" Jessie asked coyly, her fingers teasing at the edge of her bra.

Harvey was on her in an instant, his hands eager and impatient. He tore her dress open, ripping the buttons right from their seams. Harvey the milkman, usually so reserved and respectful, had been unleashed, and Jessie loved every second of it.

She pulled his face to hers and kissed him hard, their tongues exploring each other's mouths with a desperate need. Harvey's hands were everywhere, cupping her breasts, squeezing her ass, pulling her closer. They were both burning with desire, consumed by an insatiable lust that could only be quenched by the other's touch.

Jessie moaned as Harvey's lips found her neck, kissing and sucking at the delicate skin there. She knew he would leave marks, but she didn't care; in fact, she wanted him to. She wanted everyone to know what a slut she was.

Jessie's hands fumbled with Harvey's belt, her fingers trembling with anticipation. She finally managed to undo it, and she quickly unzipped his pants, freeing his erection from the confines of his clothes. She gasped at the sight of it, thick and hard and ready for her.

"Is this what you like?" Harvey grunted, grabbing Jessie's breast hard enough to leave a bruise. "You like to spread your legs like a little whore while your husband is at work? You like to fuck the milkman like a cheap slut?"

Jessie could only moan in response, too aroused to form words. Harvey's crude words and rough actions only fueled her desire, and she wanted nothing more than to feel him inside her.

"You're a dirty girl, Jessie. I can't believe you're letting me do this to you. I'm going to fuck you so hard you won't be able to walk straight for a week," Harvey growled, his fingers sliding through her wetness. "And then, maybe, you'll stop trying to seduce me every time I deliver your milk."

Jessie cried out as Harvey thrust two fingers inside her, stretching her tight pussy. She arched her back, grinding against his hand, desperate for more.

Harvey's lips moved to her ear, his voice low and husky. "You're so wet, Jessie. I think you like it when I talk to you like that. I think you like being a dirty little slut."

Jessie could only whimper in agreement, her body aching with need. She reached for Harvey's cock, stroking it slowly, feeling the heat of his desire in her hand.

Harvey groaned and pulled his fingers from her pussy, bringing them to her mouth. "Suck them clean," he ordered, pressing them against her lips.

Jessie eagerly complied, licking and sucking her juices from his fingers, the taste of her own arousal fueling her lust even further.

Harvey watched her with a mix of awe and hunger, his eyes dark with desire. "That's a good girl. You like the way you taste, don't you? You're going to swallow every drop when I come inside your filthy little mouth. I'm going to smear that cheap red lipstick all over your face while you choke on my cock."

Jessie moaned and nodded, eager to please. She sank to her knees, ready to take him in her mouth. Harvey's hands grabbed her hair, pulling her closer.

Just when Jessie was about to take Harvey as deep into her throat as she could, she heard the crash of the front door slamming.

"What the fuck is this?" her husband Luke's voice boomed across the kitchen. "What the hell is going on here?"

Jessie pulled away from Harvey's cock, shocked and afraid. She looked up at her husband, tears welling in her eyes. "I... I... It's not what it looks like, I swear! It just... happened..."

Luke was livid, his face contorted with rage. "How dare you? How fucking dare you! You filthy little whore! I should have listened to my mother; she was right about you. You're only good for one thing, and that's spreading your legs for any man who comes along."

Jessie was trembling, tears streaming down her face. She felt ashamed and guilty, but she also felt a strange sense of exhilaration.

"Baby," she crawled to her husband on her hands and knees. "You're right. I'm a filthy little whore. I'm sorry. Please let me make it up to you. Let me show you how sorry I am."

She slowly began to unbuckle Luke's belt, her hands shaking with anticipation. He stood there, silent and stoic, his eyes burning with anger. She pulled his pants down and freed his erection, hard and ready for her.

"Harvey, watch as I swallow my husband's cock," Jessie said over her shoulder. "Watch as I take him all the way into my throat. Watch as he fucks my face like a cheap whore."

Jessie didn't wait for Harvey's response before taking her husband's cock into her mouth, tasting the salty tang of his pre-come on her tongue. She swirled her tongue around the head, teasing and taunting him, before taking him deeper into her throat.

Luke groaned, his hands fisting in her hair. "Is this what you want, you little slut? You want to suck my cock while another man watches?"

Jessie moaned in response, her mouth full of her husband's cock. She could feel Harvey's eyes on her, watching her every move, and she could see him from the corner of her eye, grinning as she stroked his cock, still wet from her mouth.

Luke fucked her mouth with a brutal intensity, his thrusts punctuated by grunts of pleasure and frustration. "You're such a fucking whore, Jessie. Look at you, getting off on sucking my cock in front of another man."

Jessie whimpered, her pussy dripping wet as she took her husband's cock deeper into her throat. She wanted nothing more than to feel a fat cock inside her, but she knew that she would have to wait.

Luke's grip on her hair tightened as he thrust his hips forward, burying himself deep inside her mouth.

"I think I need to teach you a lesson," Luke growled, gripping his wife's hair and watching the eyeliner drip down her cheeks. "One man not enough for you? You want two men? Well, I'll give you two. You can take it all at once, you cheap slut. Split you wide open."

Harvey grinned, stroking his cock as he watched the scene unfold. Luke dragged Jessie to the sofa in the living room by her hair. He unbuttoned his own shirt and pulled down his pants before sitting on the middle cushion of the sofa, legs spread. His cock was fully erect and ready for her.

"Sit on it," Luke commanded. "Sit on my cock and show Harvey how much you can take."

Jessie climbed on top of her husband and began to slowly lower herself onto his cock, gasping as she felt him stretch her tight pussy.

"That's it, you cheap slut. Take it all in. Show Harvey what a dirty little whore you are," Luke groaned, his hands gripping her hips.

Jessie's moans filled the air as she rode her husband's cock, her pussy taking him in deeper and deeper with each thrust. She glanced at Harvey, who was watching them intently, his cock in his hand.

"So you wanna fuck my wife?" Luke barked at Harvey. "Well, she's all yours, milkman. Come over here and fuck her brains out. Take her tight little ass, she always squeals when I try. But she wants two men, she's getting two men. "

Harvey didn't need to be told twice. He approached the married couple on the sofa, his cock rock-hard and ready for action. Jessie felt a jolt of excitement as Harvey positioned himself behind her, rubbing his cock against her asshole. She gasped as she felt the pressure of his cock begin to stretch her tight hole, the unfamiliar sensation sending waves of pleasure through her body.

As Harvey's cock slowly entered her ass, Jessie let out a cry of pleasure. She had never felt so full, so complete. She couldn't believe she was being fucked in both holes by two men at once.

"Oh god, oh god!" she cried out, her head thrown back in ecstasy.

Luke held her hips as she bounced up and down on his cock, his thrusts matching Harvey's. "That's it, you little whore. Take it all in. You wanted two cocks? Now you've got two cocks. You're going to feel us both come inside you, you filthy little slut. We're going to fill you up."

Jessie cried out as the two men stretched her to her limits, filling her up in a way she never had been before. She didn't know how much she could take, but at this point she also knew that she couldn't stop them from using her body, no matter how hard they fucked her.

"Please... please... please..." she moaned, her body rocking with the force of their thrusts. She wasn't sure if she was begging them to stop or begging them to keep going.

Luke's grip on her hips tightened as his thrusts grew more urgent. "Come on, milkman, you're gonna make me do all the work? I thought you wanted to fuck my wife."

Harvey grunted and began to thrust harder, his cock sliding in and out of Jessie's tight ass with a slick wet sound. "Fuck, she feels so good. Her ass is so tight, I can barely stand it."

Jessie felt her orgasm building, and she knew it wouldn't be long before she came. "Oh god, oh god, I'm gonna come! I'm gonna come!" she cried out, her voice hoarse with pleasure.

"That's right, you little whore," her husband shoved two fingers into her mouth. "I bet you wish we had a third guy here. Or maybe I should just invite all the guys from work over to have a go at you. Would you like that? A whole room full of men fucking you? Using you like the cheap whore you are?"

Jessie couldn't speak, her body overwhelmed with pleasure as the two men continued to fuck her relentlessly. She felt Harvey's cock pulsing inside her ass, and she knew he was close to coming. She felt her own orgasm building, and she knew it was going to be explosive.

"Come on, milkman, finish her off. I want to see her come all over my cock while she takes yours up her ass," Luke growled, his thrusts becoming more erratic.

Harvey groaned and quickened his pace, his thrusts growing more forceful and urgent. "Fuck, I'm gonna come," he panted, his hands gripping Jessie's hips as he pounded into her tight ass.

As Harvey's cock throbbed and pulsed inside her, Jessie felt her own orgasm wash over her. Her body shuddered and convulsed as she screamed in pleasure, her pussy clenching around Luke's cock as she came.

Luke's thrusts grew faster and deeper as he felt his wife's orgasm. He gripped her hips tightly as he fucked her, grunting and groaning as he approached his own climax.

"Take it, you cheap slut," he growled as he buried his cock deep inside her, his hot come filling her up.

Harvey pulled out of Jessie's ass, his come dripping from her gaping hole as he stood back to admire his handiwork. "Damn, that was a good fuck," he said with a satisfied grin.

Jessie lay there, spent and exhausted, her body still quivering from the intensity of her orgasm. She couldn't believe what she had just done, what she had let two men do to her, but she knew that she had never felt more alive.

"That was incredible," she whispered, her voice hoarse and raw. "I've never felt anything like that before."

Luke smirked as he gently stroked his wife's hair. "You like being a dirty little whore, don't you? Well, maybe you were right. Maybe two men is better than one. Maybe we'll have to do this again sometime."

Harvey laughed and slapped Jessie on the ass. "Damn right we will. You got a tight ass, lady. And I want more of it."

Jessie looked up at the two men, her body trembling with anticipation and desire. She couldn't believe that her dull, monotonous life had suddenly been turned upside down, and she knew that she would never be the same again.

* * *

SHARING MY WIFE WITH THE COP

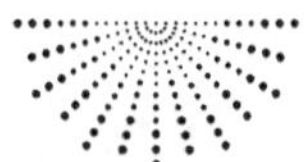

* * *

The morning sun filtered through the dense canopy, casting a kaleidoscope of shadows on the narrow trail. Newlyweds Emilia and Harry, hand in hand, wandered off the beaten path, their laughter echoing in the serene wilderness. The air was alive with the chirps of hidden birds and the rustle of leaves underfoot.

"Race you to the clearing!" Harry challenged, a mischievous glint in his eyes.

Emilia's laughter bubbled up as she darted ahead, "You're on!"

Their footsteps were light, almost dancing over roots and rocks. As they reached a sun-dappled clearing, surrounded by towering pines and wildflowers, Emilia playfully collapsed onto the soft grass, pulling Harry down beside her.

"Caught you!" Harry exclaimed, his breath mingling with hers.

Emilia gazed into his eyes, those familiar pools of warmth, and whispered, "You always do."

"So," Harry's eyes sparkled with a mischievous glint, "what do I win? A kiss?"

Emilia couldn't help the giggle that escaped her. Harry's playfulness was contagious.

As he leaned in closer, she teased, "Only if you can catch me."

Emily rolled over and tried to dart away but Harry caught her by her hips and pulled her back to him.

"Caught you again," Harry murmured, rubbing his swelling cock against his wife's firm backside. "And that's twice. Now I think you owe me a little more than a kiss."

Emilia felt her pussy throb as Harry slipped his hand through the leg of her shorts, reaching for her panties. His fingers slipped beneath the cotton, finding her already wet.

"Already so wet," Harry purred in her ear, his finger circling her clit. "What a naughty girl."

"Harry!" Emilia protested softly, wiggling her ass against Harry's hardening cock. "We're in public!"

Harry let out a low growl, biting his bottom lip as he pushed aside the thin fabric of her panties. He rubbed his bare fingers over her dripping cunt, coating his digits in her slick before sliding one finger inside her. Emilia gasped as Harry began to fuck her with his fingers, adding a second digit as she squirmed and moaned beneath him.

"There's nobody out here," Harry whispered, his other hand pushing up Emilia's shirt and unhooking her bra. "Come on, baby, let me hear those pretty sounds. You're so wet. No one will ever know."

Emilia moaned softly, her hands finding Harry's, as she ground her hips against him. She could feel his cock, hard and insistent, pressing into her ass.

"Harry... please," Emilia breathed, her eyes closed, as Harry continued to fuck her with his fingers. "We should go back to the lodge."

"The lodge is a two hour hike back down the moun-tain," Harry chided. "I can feel you want it, Em. Just let me do this to you. Relax."

Emilia whimpered but she also thrust her pussy back onto Harry's fingers. She couldn't help it, it felt so good. Plus, Harry was right. They hadn't seen a single soul on the entire trail. They were definitely not at serious risk of getting caught.

Harry chuckled softly, his breath tickling her ear, "You want me to fuck you right here in the middle of the forest?"

Emilia nodded, unable to deny that she did.

Harry pressed his thumb against Emilia's clit and rubbed in slow, tight circles. Emilia let out a moan, her hips bucking as Harry's fingers curled inside her, finding the most sensitive part of her pussy.

"Such a naughty girl," Harry whispered. "So naughty."

Emilia nodded again, her breath coming in shallow gasps as Harry increased the speed of his fingers, fucking her harder. The palm of his hand slapped against her ass as he thrust his fingers into her, making her wetter and wetter.

"Harry..." Emilia groaned, her pussy throbbing, "I'm close."

Harry pressed his thumb harder against her clit, increasing the pressure as he finger fucked her faster. He whispered in her ear, his voice low and husky, "Come for me, baby."

Emilia felt her orgasm building inside her, the pressure becoming unbearable. She arched her back, her hips bucking, as she cried out, her pussy clenching around Harry's fingers.

"Good girl," Harry murmured, his fingers still moving inside her. "Such a good girl."

Emilia whimpered as Harry pulled his fingers out of her cunt, his other hand massaging her ass.

"Now let's just pull these down," Harry pulled Emilia's shorts and panties from her hips, revealing her round ass and her wet, pink pussy.

Emilia moaned as she felt Harry's cock brush against her slick cunt lips, teasing her.

"Harry..." she breathed, her thighs trembling.

Harry grinned as he pushed his cock into Emilia's tight hole, sliding in easily, her arousal allowing him to bottom out with a single thrust.

"Oh god!" Emilia moaned, her pussy clenching around Harry's thick cock.

Harry gripped Emilia's hips and began to fuck her, hard and fast.

Emilia moaned loudly as Harry slammed his cock into her, filling her completely. She reached out to grab the grass beneath her, twisting the cool blades in her hands as Harry pounded her pussy.

"You feel so good," Harry growled, his fingers digging into her hips.

Emilia pushed back against Harry, meeting each thrust with her own, her pussy soaking his cock. Harry groaned, his fingers gripping her ass, as he continued to fuck her, their bodies moving together in the soft grass, under the summer sun.

"Freeze!" an angry voice came from the edge of the clearing.

"Fuck," Harry whipped around in shock, inadvertently pulling his cock from his wife's wet, swollen pussy.

He stared up into the barrel of a revolver.

"Hands where I can see them!" the cop shouted, his voice cold and harsh. "Now!"

Harry put his hands up, his cock still throbbing.

Emilia squeaked in fright and turned her head, trying to look back over her shoulder at the man who was pointing a gun at her and her husband.

"Ma'am," the cop addressed her without taking his eyes off Harry, "was this man assaulting you? Do you require medical assistance?"

"Assaulting?" Emilia was caught off guard, her shorts still around her knees. "No, this is my husband. We were just..."

"Having a little fun?" the cop rolled his eyes and lowered his gun. "You two know you aren't in your backyard right now? This is a public trail. People bring their children here. You could have been seen by any number of hikers. What were you thinking?"

Harry swallowed hard, his cock twitching as Emilia's glistening pussy stared up at him.

"I'm sorry, officer," he began, "we didn't think anyone was going to be up here."

"Well you thought wrong," the cop replied. "You're lucky I was the only one to find you. You know this is illegal? If a family had run into this, that could be a child abuse charge. As things stand, I'm going to have to write you both up on public obscenity," the cops eyes drifted over Emilia's wet pussy. "Too bad, really, a young couple like you. You'll probably both have to register as sex offenders."

"No!" Emilia cried out. "Please, officer. Please don't do that. I'm a kindergarten teacher. I'll lose my job!"

"Well," the cop shook his head, still unable to take his eyes off of Emilia's body, "you should have thought of that before you--"

"Wait," Emilia noticed the cop checking her out. "Isn't there any way we could..."

"Could what?" the cop raised an eyebrow.

"Emilia!" Harry laughed.

"Any way we could..." Emilia gave her best pout.

"Any way you could what?" the cop grinned, adjusting his swelling cock in his trousers.

"We could come to some sort of... arrangement?" Emilia suggested.

The cop laughed, "You want me to let you go without writing you up?"

Emilia nodded, biting her lip, "Maybe."

The cop walked around to face Emilia. "And how do you think you could convince me to do that?"

Emilia smiled up at the cop, her eyes drifting to the bulge in his pants. "I can think of a few ways. Like maybe you could... I don't know. Just punish me yourself?"

The cop grinned, "Punish you?"

"Mmhm," Emilia nodded. "I've been such a naughty girl. I think you should spank me."

"Emilia!" Harry laughed.

"Spank you?" the cop raised an eyebrow. "You're a married woman."

Emilia smiled, "I am. But Harry won't mind if you do it. Harry already knows what a bad girl I am. In fact, this was all my idea. I got him in trouble too."

"Is that so?" the cop chuckled, shaking his head. "I can't believe I'm even considering this. You do realize that I could have you both arrested and charged with public indecency? And bribery?"

"I know," Emilia nodded. "But I also know that I look good."

Emilia spread her legs, pushing her ass into the air, "And I can tell that you think so too."

"Alright," the cop sighed, unzipping his pants, "if you insist. But I'm only doing this because you asked for it and I don't want a little fun to ruin your entire lives."

"Thank you," Emilia whispered.

The cop looked over at Harry, "You okay with this, man?"

Harry shrugged, "As long as Emilia's happy. Go ahead."

"Okay," the cop grinned, "I'm going to give you ten smacks. Count them out loud. Understood?"

"Yes, officer," Emilia nodded. "I understand."

The cop raised his hand and brought it down on Emilia's ass with a resounding smack.

"One!" Emilia counted.

The cop grinned and spanked her again, this time on the other cheek.

"Two!" Emilia winced.

The cop continued to spank Emilia's ass, counting along with her, until she reached ten.

"Ten," Emilia breathed, her ass red and sore.

The cop grinned, rubbing his cock. "You took that very well. But I'm not sure you've learned your lesson."

"Please," Emilia whined, "I'll be good."

The cop shook his head, "Not yet. I think I need to give you a few more."

"No," Emilia pleaded, "please don't."

"Well I can't just let you go without making sure that you've learned your lesson," the cop replied. "And I'm still pretty worked up from seeing you two fucking like animals in the middle of the forest."

Emilia whimpered softly, her ass burning.

"Tell you what," the cop offered. "If you make me cum, I'll let you both go free."

"Make you cum?" Emilia asked.

The cop nodded, pulling his cock out of his pants. His cock was thick and long, with a slight curve to it.

"Suck it," the cop commanded.

Emilia stared at the cop's cock, unsure of whether to do as he said. She glanced over at Harry who shrugged and smiled, already stroking his own cock at the sight of his wife's tender red ass.

"Alright," Emilia nodded, "but I've never done this before. With two guys, I mean."

"That's okay," the cop grinned, "I'm sure you'll do fine."

Emilia leaned forward and took the cop's cock into her mouth, sucking on the tip. The cop groaned, his cock throbbing against her lips. Emilia continued to suck his cock, her tongue running along the length of it.

"Jesus," the cop groaned, "you're so fucking good at this. I bet you're even better at taking cock. Why don't you show me how good you are at taking your husband's cock? You must love it when he fucks you."

Emilia moaned, the vibrations of her voice causing the cop to groan again. Emilia released the cop's cock with a pop and smiled up at him.

"I love it when Harry fucks me," Emilia admitted. "But I love sucking cock too. Especially yours."

The cop laughed, "Well I'm glad to hear that. Now get back to work."

Emilia returned to sucking the cop's cock, her hands cupping his balls. The cop groaned, his hips thrusting as he fucked Emilia's mouth. Emilia gagged slightly as the cop's cock hit the back of her throat.

"That's it," the cop encouraged. "Take it all."

Emilia relaxed her throat and took the cop's cock deeper, her eyes watering slightly. She bobbed her head up and down, sucking hard.

Meanwhile, Harry lined the head of his cock up with his wife's wet, throbbing pussy and slid inside her with one smooth thrust. Emilia moaned around the cop's cock, her pussy clenching around Harry's cock.

Harry began to fuck Emilia slowly, his cock sliding in and out of her wet cunt. The cop groaned as Emilia continued to suck his cock, her tongue running along the underside of his shaft.

"Fuck," the cop moaned. "You two are wild. I don't know how I'm going to be able to let you both go after this."

Emilia sucked the cop's cock harder, her tongue swirling around the tip. Harry continued to fuck her, his cock hitting her g-spot with each thrust. Emilia moaned, the vibrations from her voice sending shivers through the cop's body.

"Alright," the cop sighed, pulling his cock from Emilia's mouth. "That's enough of that. Let's see what you can do with that tight pussy."

The cop looked over at Harry who had stopped fucking Emilia and was simply holding his cock inside her.

"You heard me," the cop said, "I want to see how well she takes your cock."

Harry grinned and resumed fucking Emilia, his cock slamming into her tight pussy. Emilia moaned, her pussy clenching around Harry's cock as he fucked her.

"Oh fuck," Harry groaned, his hips bucking as he fucked Emilia. "I'm close."

"Come inside her," the cop instructed.

Harry groaned and thrust his cock deep inside Emilia, his balls slapping against her ass as he came, filling her with his hot cum. Emilia cried out as she reached her own orgasm, her pussy clenching around Harry's cock as she came.

"Fuck," Harry breathed, his cock still throbbing inside Emilia.

The cop laughed and shook his head. "Well, I guess you're done then. But I'm not."

"I thought you said you'd let us go if I made you cum," Emilia panted.

The cop smirked, "I said I'd let you go if you made me cum with your mouth. And I've changed my mind about that. You didn't make me cum, so you'll have to find another way to convince me."

"What do you want me to do?" Emilia asked, her pussy still throbbing around Harry's cock.

"I want to fuck you," the cop replied, stroking his cock. "I want to fuck your tight little pussy."

Emilia nodded, "Okay. Just be gentle."

The cop laughed, "Don't worry, I won't break you."

He positioned himself behind Emilia and slid his cock into her wet, cum-filled pussy. Emilia moaned as the cop's thick cock filled her, stretching her tight pussy. Harry watched in fascination as his wife's pussy was stretched by the cop's cock.

"Fuck," the cop groaned as he began to fuck Emilia, "your pussy is so tight. I can feel your husband's cum inside you."

Emilia moaned as the cop fucked her, his cock sliding in and out of her pussy. She gripped the grass beneath her as the cop fucked her hard, his cock slamming into her wet pussy.

"You like that, don't you?" the cop grunted as he fucked Emilia. "You like being fucked by two men at the same time."

"Yes," Emilia moaned, her pussy clenching around the cop's cock as she came.

"Fuck," the cop groaned, "you're so fucking tight. I'm going to cum soon."

"Please," Emilia begged, "cum inside me."

"Fuck," the cop growled, his cock throbbing as he came inside Emilia, filling her with his cum.

Emilia cried out as she reached her own orgasm, her pussy clenching around the cop's cock as she came. Harry watched in awe as Emilia came, her pussy clenching around the cop's cock as she came.

The cop pulled out of Emilia and took a step back, his cock still throbbing. Emilia collapsed onto the ground, panting, her legs spread and her pussy dripping with cum. Harry sat down beside her, stroking her hair.

"So," the cop asked, "did you learn your lesson? Will you be more careful about where you decide to have sex in the future?"

Emilia nodded, unable to speak.

Harry laughed, "I think she did, officer. Thanks for not writing us up."

The cop grinned, "No problem. Just remember, I'm watching you. If I ever see you two fucking in public again, you're both going to jail. Understood?"

Emilia nodded, still unable to speak.

The cop shook his head and laughed, "Alright. Well, I guess I'll be on my way. You two have a nice day."

Emilia and Harry watched as the cop walked away, disappearing into the forest. Emilia looked up at Harry and smiled, her eyes sparkling with mischief.

"What?" Harry asked, raising an eyebrow.

"Do you think we could get away with a quickie in the car before we go back to the lodge?" Emilia giggled.

Harry laughed and shook his head, "I think we're pushing our luck, Em. Maybe next time."

Emilia pouted, "Fine. But I'm going to hold you to that, Harry. Next time we go on a trip, we're having sex in the car. Deal?"

"Deal," Harry agreed. "Now let's get back to the lodge before we really get in trouble."

Emilia and Harry gathered their clothes and headed back down the trail, hand in hand.

* * *

BONUS: SHARING THE LANDLADY

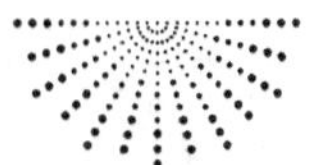

* * *

"Where's the friggin key Bryan?"

"Wait, I thought you had it…"

"…Naah man, last man out was you."

"God not this shit again. I swear to god man, you're long overdue a CT scan. I gave you the key right before we went into Katie's party remember?"

"And why would you do that?"

"You've got Alzheimer's or something mate… Because we, me and you, came to the conclusion that between the two of us, *you* were the responsible one."

"Fuck!"

"Yup. 'Fuck' sounds just about right. Want me to look up cheap brain scan alternatives?"

"No Stupid, somebody's gonna have to wake Addy up."

"FUCK!"

"Ya think?"

Elijah and Bryan had gone through this scenario multiple times before. Losing the keys to their apartment was a normal Friday night with them. Bryan had come up with the ingenious idea mandating that Elijah, or Eli as he loved to call him, be the chief custodian of said keys. Granted this didn't much change things, but at least there was a clear chain of command. In most instances, Bryan was the 'key-tossing' culprit, and as such, it was he that ended up knocking on Addison's door at 4 O'clock in the morning. Addison was their 40-year-old landlady, and man did she hate their antics. She threatened to chuck them onto the street every time they crossed paths. Incidentally, they had yet to pay rent for the month, and this Friday was the fifth day of said month. So much for responsibility.

Eli and Bryan sat in silent contemplation of their actions these past months. There were times when

Bryan saw the light (often after a thorough night's party and a consequent bout of early morning nausea) and made guilt-fed, in-the-moment decisions to never again indulge in the plain vanities of the world. But these insincere bouts of conviction were rare, and in most cases, they didn't last very long. Eli was, on the other hand, the voice of reason, muffled almost always, but still the voice of reason. He'd known Bryan all his life, and they'd always gone through the expected motions together. Middle-school dances, Prom, Girlfriends, Sex, everything. Admittedly, Bryan was not a good influence on him. But he couldn't just jump ship… Right?

"She'll fucking kick us out man, I just know it." Eli said to Bryan who was seated on the floor, his back to the door.

"Just tell her you tossed the key man, that always works with me…" Bryan offered.

"Yeah what happens when she asks about rent then?"

"Don't think about it too much, that's how you jinx it."

"I swear to god man, I don't know how you do it. Alright, here goes." Eli started up the stairs and then turned back instantly.

"What the hell man, no defaulting on your own rules."Bryan stood up and grabbed Eli by the shoulders, turning him around and pushing him up the stairs.

"Come on Bryan, help a brother out." Eli begged.

"Naah this one's on you. No turning back." Bryan patted his uncertain friend on the shoulder and gave him a solid push onto the landing toward his fears.

Eli tried to think of what he'd tell Addy but all that crossed before his eyes was a bunch of indecipherable gibberish. His imagination wasn't wild, but it was reliable… as far as he could tell. He could definitely come up with a solid lie, or could he? He tried to visualize how Addy would react, from what little he could tell from Bryan's interactions with her, which wasn't much at all (Bryan seemingly wasn't scared of her), Addy wouldn't much appreciate a courtesy call at… He glanced down at the watch on his wrist… 3:27 a.m.

"Fuck!" He had finally made it to her door. The number of times he'd knocked on that door he could count on one hand. Scratch that, he'd knocked on it twice; that first week after they'd moved in when he was asking about the air conditioning, and once when *he'd* lost the keys himself (almost a year ago) and neither time had been pretty.

"Fuck me." Eli stretched out his arm and rapped slightly on the door. No reply. He knocked harder and listened for sound inside the apartment, wondering what would happen if she hadn't heard him, or worse, if she had. He raised his arm again, intending on unleashing one last solid bunch of thumps upon the door when it swung open.

"I swear to fucking god Bryan, if you've lost..." Addy stood in the doorway, her mouth opened in a small pout, the half-said threat hanging in the uncertain air between her and the towering college kid that rented the apartment below her's.

"What on earth are you doing knocking on my door at such an ungodly hour?" She said, regaining her composure. Eli didn't seem to hear her query as he stared at her. Addison looked a hell of a lot different. Eli stared amazedly at her perfect body, glowing under the silky chiffon nightdress she wore, taking in all the changes. The night dress just about reached her knees, and the flimsy material was such that he could see her nipples outlined clearly. Feeling self-conscious under Eli's lustful stare, Addy wrapped her arms around her torso and crossed her legs, and ended up standing at a weird angle. Right then, Eli realized his folly and looked away almost instantly,

"I'm sorry... Uhh... I...Uhm. I lost the keys to the... Uhm... the apartment, and I was hoping you could maybe help us out?"

Addy looked at him for a short while, as if considering what to do with him, and then she turned around and walked back into her apartment, leaving the door open. Eli looked up and saw Addy disappear behind a sliding door in the apartment. Then as he contemplated his next move,

"You gonna keep standing there or you wanna come in?"

Eli lingered in the doorway for a minute, skeptical, like he was a vampire and the invite was a clever play on words, and he'd go up in flames the minute he walked through the doorway. And then, seeing no other play, he walked into the apartment and locked the door behind him.

* * *

Bryan felt his ass grow numb from sitting so long on the floor. How long had it been? He wondered to himself. It was taking Eli all fucking night to get the spares from Addy. Had he chickened out? No way, Eli wasn't that type of guy. Plus, Bryan reasoned, he'd heard him bang on the door like a friggin madman a while ago. Addy sure as hell won't like that, he thought to himself. Then out loud,

"I wonder what he'll think of Addison's smashing bod."

* * *

Eli stood awkwardly by the open kitchen counter, not daring to touch either of the bar stools beneath it and as close to the door as possible. He'd had such a dream before; he gets invited into a stranger's house in the middle of the night, and then suddenly he's the victim of some twisted serial killer, his picture strewn all over the internet, images and videos of his distorted person being circulated on the dark web amongst losers, trolls, and possible psychopaths...

"You wanna sit down?" Addy said, interrupting his morbid thoughts. She now wore a huge bathrobe over the nightdress, effectively covering her beautiful body from Eli's predator-like stare.

"Uuh... Yeah, sure." Eli replied and walked toward the couch.

"So... Rent." Addy started. She'd pulled one of the tall stools from beneath the extended kitchen counter and was perched upon it like a Mafioso lady boss. Her body was hidden from view, all except her crossed leg, exposed as if jutting out for air. Eli struggled to hold her gaze; he'd known that rent would be a part of the conversation, but he'd at least hoped that Addy would've been too sleepy to focus much on it. Shock on him. What made it worse was that whenever he looked away, his gaze was immediately drawn toward her magnificent legs. Fuck! He thought to himself.

"I'll sort you out as soon as possible…" He started.

"Wait what? You don't even have this month's payment? God, I'm here thinking we're talking about how you're always late on your deposits, and here you are telling me to wait some…"

She didn't sound particularly angry at Eli, and he didn't know why, but at that moment, he went all out,

"Come on Addy, don't stress… I'm sure we could work something out…"

"Like what?" Addy took him up on his cryptic offer, her thoughts way ahead of his.

"I don't know… we could do some odd jobs for you, fix stuff around the house… whatever you've got in mind."

Addy slowly got off her stool, her mouth curled in a wicked smile, and sauntered toward Eli, "Odd jobs huh?"

* * *

"Fuck!" Bryan jolted out of the uncomfortable sleep he'd slowly drifted into. He'd dozed off for a minute and this time round, he was fairly certain Eli had bolted and left him to face up to Addy. Whatever type of guy he was, Bryan was really angry with him. He stood up from his miserable made-up bed on the floor and started up the stairs.

"I'll fucking show him." Bryan thought as he cleared the top stair and walked down the hallway toward Addison's apartment. He got to the door and seeing it slightly open, pushed and walked into the apartment, his jaw dropping as he did.

Eli's turned around from whatever it was he was preoccupied with and caught Bryan's unbelieving gaze, and then a wicked grin tore across his face.

Bryan stared back at Eli and a similar smile shone his face up. Right on Eli! He thought approvingly. Eli was holding Addy's hands behind her, and she was bent over on the couch, her head buried deep in the

Chesterfield, her back bent in a magnificent arch, juxtaposing her sexy ass perfectly against Eli's hairy crotch. Both of them were naked and from how Addy was moaning, it seemed they'd been so a while. Then Addy, as if sensing that a third party had crossed over the threshold and into her apartment, raised her head and caught sight of Bryan.

"Don't stop on my account." Bryan said, a weird attempt at humor.

"Well don't just stand there," Addison replied, brushing aside Bryan's sarcasm, "make yourself useful."

Bryan didn't waste time taking Addy up on her offer and in mere seconds, he had taken off all of his clothing. He took a minute to carefully lock the door behind him lest some other guy stumbles upon that there goldmine and spoils all the fun.

Eli and Bryan had seen each other naked on many occasions before. What they'd never actually done was share a meal (speaking in metaphorical sexual terms). Luckily enough for them, Addy wasn't about to let either of them fuck this up for her.

"Come on Honey I'll show you where to put it." She offered. Bryan took Addy's hand and let her lead him to the couch where he settled comfortably. Addy widened her stance, slightly spreading her legs apart, and bent over like a yoga master, or some other flexible compatriot. She took Bryan's dick into her mouth and started sucking on it like mad. Eli, feeling a tad more comfortable, decided to take a more novel approach to his 7 minutes of fame. He got down to his knees and, grabbing Addy's outer thighs, started weaving an intricate web of slob and musky precum all over her inner thighs, slowly circling his target, bidding his time until the perfect moment to attack came.

Bryan felt Addy's head jerk up and down his pulsing penis expertly, and he wondered how in the hell Eli had talked Addy into this. He opened his eyes momentarily and saw Addy draw the hair away from her face. He stretched out his arm and gently took a chunk of Addy's hair into his hand. He applied the tiniest bit of pressure and Addy seemed to yield beneath it. Does she want me all rough and shit, Bryan wondered to himself. Well, there was only one way to find out. He yanked her head back and looked her straight in the eyes. Yes, that is definitely what she wants, he concluded. He leaned in low and kissed her lips. Addy kissed him back, suddenly drawing back, and letting out a squeaky scream. She smiled at him as a drop of blood trailed down her lip. Bryan had finally figured her out. He slapped her face and roughly shoved his dick back inside her slobbery mouth.

Meanwhile, Eli was carefully plotting out all of Addy's pleasure points (subconsciously). He saw Bryan wink at him from the corner of his eye and immediately knew that something was up. He stood up and shoved his dick back inside Addy's pussy. He wanted to know what it was Bryan was gesturing about.

Bryan grabbed Addy's hair harder and forced himself deep inside her throat, lingering there for a moment, before letting Addy come up for air.

"You wanna choke on me some more?" Bryan asked.

"Yes." Addy replied.

"Yes Baby!" Bryan ordered.

"Yes Baby, I wanna choke on that there monster." Addy replied sensually, her voice barely a whisper.

She enjoyed the attention Bryan and Eli were giving her. It was like a scene from one of her favorite porn flicks. And she was the submissive bitch getting ruthlessly spit-roasted by two sexy college kids. Her thighs shook as she thought about it.

Eli finally caught on. He stopped the gentle touches and rhythmic thrusts. Instantly, he had turned into an animal. He thrust himself deep inside Addy's pussy, spanking her hard as he did. Addy moaned in pleasure, the sounds getting mixed up with the sticky noises from Bryan's mad blowjob. Suddenly, Eli pulled out of her and then, shoving two fingers into her gaping pussy, grabbed her neck, and flipped her onto the couch like she was cutlery. The two guys towered above her, each set on a destination.

Eli grabbed her head and glaring down at her, shoved his dick inside her mouth. Addy lay flat on her back and both her legs were spread out wide, divulging the contents of her juicy cunt. He held her head with both hands, and then he thrust himself inside her mouth like she was a thing incapable of feeling fear, or pain, or disgust. Her sole purpose; to offer and receive pleasure. He thrust so hard that his balls slapped at her forehead.

Bryan took his dick in his hand and slid it along her wet vagina, teasing her as he did. He bent over and tasted her for himself; god she smelt good, he thought. And then he noticed it. Her taut untouched anus. This was going to be fun. He licked her clit and slobbered all over her groin. He spit in his hand, and then rubbing the tip of his penis, pretended to lead it into her cunt.

Addy's eyes grew wide with elated disbelief. Her hands flailed all over, but she was effectively stuck. Her hips arched sharply to try and accommodate the bulging dick that violated her anus. She wanted to cry, but why the hell it felt so good, she did not understand. Her previously spread-eagled legs tried to instinctively come together to help prevent whatever sorcery was going on in her pelvis, but they failed miserably. Bryan's muscular arms pinned them in place, leaving her to his mercy. She moaned from the unrelenting mix of pain and pleasure that was fucking up her system, but Eli's dick had effectively taken up residency in her throat, probably messing with her phalanx, what with all that girth.

Bryan started with slow gentle thrusts, but the unbelievable grip with which Addy's ass choked his pulsing dick made it too hard to resist. He shoved harder with each passing second. He could literally feel her milk the cum out of him.

Eli felt Addy's mouth slacken as her mind became preoccupied with the magic that was going on down below. He wrapped a hand around her neck and slowly tightened his grip.

Addy felt herself drift in and out of consciousness; was she about to faint? No, that wasn't it. She was walking the line between sanity and the fiery all-consuming power of sexual deviancy. The line between pleasure and pain. And then as if that wasn't enough, Addy felt Eli's other hand trace its way slowly. Starting from her supple breasts, flowing to her navel, and then lingering for a while around her lower abdomen, building suspense, before firmly shoving its fingers inside her pulsing womanhood. Up until then, Addy had thought, this is as far as I can get. It has got to be. There's no greater checkpoint. Until there was. It was like nothing she could ever imagine, like, like… It was like meeting God, and then meeting her mother. It was mind-blowing.

Eli rubbed at Addy's exposed clit with one hand. The other hand tightened like a vice over her neck. Addy pursed her lips in one final act of defiance, determined to take at least one of the boys down with her.

Bryan felt Addy's anus tighten infinitely over his pulsating phallus, pushing him to the edge of ecstasy. He burst inside her ass with a maddening shiver. His limp body, devoid of every bit of strength, struggled to stay upright.

Addy felt the warm alien liquid explode deep inside her as Bryan came. Her own body, unable to take anymore, buckled in a creamy mix of sweat and cum that shook her so. Her toes curled and her hands, looking for something to grab, gripped Eli's balls tightly. Eli screamed in a twisted, otherworldly voice. A play on both pain and pleasure. He doubled over and shuddered as he emptied his load into Addy's mouth.

Ten minutes later, the three of them; Addison, Elijah, and Bryan, were still seated on the sweaty Chesterfield. All of them naked, all of them contemplating in their own way, what they had just experienced. They sat in silence for a while before Bryan broke the silence,

"Hey Eli."

"Yeah man?" Replied Elijah.

"You reckon we're good on rent?"

GET A FREE BOOK!

* * *

Be the first to find out about all of Lee Riley's new releases, book sales, and freebies by joining her VIP Mailing List. Join today and get a FREE book -- instantly!

Check Lee Riley's website spicybestsellers.com for more books.

* * *

ABOUT LEE RILEY

* * *

Lee Riley is an adventurous writer who creates spicy short stories that challenge conventions and leave readers on the edge of their seats. Drawing inspiration from their travels, Lee explores the world with insatiable curiosity, using these experiences to craft stories that captivate readers.

When not writing, Lee indulges their passion for the outdoors, discovering new culinary delights, and making connections with people from all walks of life. Their love for adventure and zest for life is reflected in their work, which is daring, unconventional, and full of surprises.

More on www.spicybestsellers.com

Contact me at lee@spicybestsellers.com

* * *

LEE RILEY
Daddy's Naughty Girls 2
DEVOURED
BY HER STEPFATHER

LEE RILEY
Daddy's Naughty Girls 3
UNDRESSED
BY HER STEPFATHER

DOMESTIC DISCIPLINE ROMANCE

LEE RILEY
6 Books! One Price!
BACK ALLEY DISCIPLINE
DOMESTIC DISCIPLINE BUNDLE

LEE RILEY
5 Books! One Price!
BACK DOOR DISCIPLINE
DOMESTIC DISCIPLINE BUNDLE

LEE RILEY
6 Books! One Price!
GET PUNISHED
DOMESTIC DISCIPLINE BUNDLE

LEE RILEY
6 Books! One Price!
GET SPANKED
DOMESTIC DISCIPLINE BUNDLE

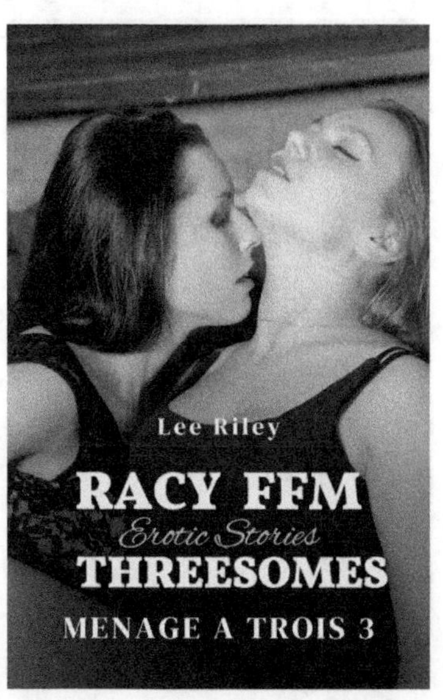

MONSTER EROTICA

LEE RILEY
MONSTROUS
ENCOUNTERS
WEREWOLVES
3 Books!
One Price!
Seductive Creatures 2

LEE RILEY
MONSTROUS
ENCOUNTERS
DEMONESSES
3 Books!
One Price!
Seductive Creatures 3

LEE RILEY
MONSTROUS ENCOUNTERS
TENTACLES & GRIM REAPER
3 Books! One Price!
Seductive Creatures 4

LEE RILEY
MONSTROUS ENCOUNTERS
KRAMPUS
Seductive Creatures 5

LEE RILEY
THE DEMON
KING
LITRPG EROTICA STORIES

* * *

www.ingramcontent.com/pod-product-compliance
Lightning Source LLC
Chambersburg PA
CBHW051343150726
48000CB00003B/1022